DARK SHIFT

PREQUEL TO THE WOLVES OF ROCK FALLS

AJ SKELLY

Quill & Flame
PUBLISHING HOUSE

QUILL & FLAME PUBLISHING HOUSE

Within these few pages, Skelly managed to make my heart ache and swoon in one sweep. -Anne J. Hill, owner of Twenty Hills Publishing

CONTENTS

The minister married me under a veil of tears. What should have been a happy moment of rejoicing was a moment of subdued sorrow. We pledged ourselves to each other and to our pack. But a piece of my heart was gone.

Because every story needs a beginning.

A NOTE FROM THE AUTHOR

Dear Reader,

Thank you so much for visiting this version of Rock Falls set in the past. This story is where everything begins—where the enmity between the two packs from *First Shift, Rogue Shift,* and *Sworn Shift* (Books One, Two, and Three of The Wolves of Rock Falls Series) is born. It's also a jumping off point for what you'll find waiting in *Pack Shift*, Book Four.

I hope you enjoy Rebekkah, Edith, Richard, and Anderson, even though their collective story is more bittersweet than some. Life is tinged with hardship and heartache, but also with hope. I hope my stories bring hope—hope that things can be different, and an escape when things are hard.

Blessings,

-AJ

CHAPTER 1

Anderson

We'd been summoned.

The Alpha of the Hawthorne pack was dying. And he had only one living heir—a she-wolf who could not inherit his title nor his pack. So, the summons went out. Every willing, eligible werewolf Alpha or Beta in the region would come to compete for the old man's lands and his pack.

And Rebekkah. I came for Rebekkah.

The trees dripped their moisture onto my head and down the back of my leather jacket. I shook my head as the wolf inside me shook his coat, anxious. My father patted his horse. Silence echoed in my chest, mixing with the nervous anticipation coursing through me.

Smoke from the settlement tickled my nose as we heeled our horses into the clearing where one large cabin and several smaller houses stood surrounding a communal fire pit and a boar roasting on a spit. Wolf licked his lips. Feeding a log onto the fire, a young woman stood. My heart lurched, and my breathing hitched. Rebekkah had blossomed in the year I'd been away. Her dark hair fell to her waist, free of her usual braid, and swung gracefully around her soft curves.

"Anderson," she whispered as joy lit her eyes. She leapt from the side of the fire pit to fling herself into my arms even before my feet were firmly planted on the ground. Father smiled and grabbed my abandoned reins.

"Rebekkah." I breathed in her sweet scent, smoke clouding her normal juniper and moss smell. She pulled back, and I reluctantly let my arms fall back to my sides, though my heart continued to pound at her nearness.

"Mr. Wolfe, thank you for coming. It will cheer my pa to see an old friend," she welcomed my father warmly.

He smiled down at her. "I will be glad to see an old friend, too. You've grown up, little wild one." His eyes held tenderness for my childhood friend.

"I have grown," she replied with a smile.

"But you are still wild?" he teased.

"You know my heart will never be tamed." Her eyes twinkled and Father chuckled. Wolf nudged me. A creature as beautiful as Rebekkah should never be tamed.

"Son, picket the horses once you've caught up with Rebekkah. Is it all right if I go into the big house to see your pa?"

"He'd be glad of the company. Edith is with him now."

Father nodded and handed me both sets of reins before walking stiffly to the cabin. The ride had been long

"I'm so glad you came. I wasn't sure who would, but I knew you and Richy would do your best to get here." Rebekkah turned to me. Her face sobered along with my heart. Richy—my other best friend from childhood—would be my competition for Rebekkah's ancestral lands...and her hand in marriage. I swallowed. Wolf whined.

"Of course, I came. How is your father?" Changing the subject kept my heart from stuttering so painfully. I flicked a piece of ash-blond hair that had fallen into my eyes.

She twisted her hands into her long skirt. "He is fading. His wolf struggles to come forth. I do not think it will be long now."

"I'm sorry, Rebekkah. Truly." Carefully, I let my fingers find her elbow. She leaned into my touch.

She gave me a watery smile. "I know. You've always understood me and how complicated it is to be the daughter of an Alpha, though you're certainly no woman yourself." She eyed me from toe to head, tipping back to look me full in the face with a saucy grin to hide her pain.

Woman I was not. At nineteen I'd been a full man for a while, but it was nice to know she'd noticed. Sometimes I wondered. I was about to remark on this but another set of hoofbeats drew our gaze to the path leading to the clearing.

Richard Woods sat tall and proud atop his snorting stallion. My heart fell to my feet as I watched Rebekkah's face take on a girlish flush that had been absent at my arrival.

"Halloo!" Richard hollered. His noise drew several others from their houses and fully into the clearing. I scuffed the toe of my boot in the dirt, knowing Richard would want an audience for his entrance.

He sidled his horse up slowly, drawing it out like a king greeting his people. His smile encompassed those who had come out their doors and he gave them a gentle wave before he fixed his attention on us.

Rebekkah fairly bounced on the balls of her feet as Richard swung his long legs down from his horse.

"Richy!" she squealed and threw herself into his arms. My excitement at seeing my friend turned to dust in my mouth. His forehead creased and he unlocked her fingers from his neck.

"Rebekkah, really. You mustn't continue calling me Richy. You must call me Richard. I've been an Alpha for three years now. I cannot let childish names follow me around," he chided. He gave her a teasing but disparaging look and chucked her quickly under her chin. My belly dropped to my toes.

"I'm sorry, I was just excited to see you," Rebekkah murmured, abashed.

"And I, you. And *you*," he turned to me. "Look at yourself, Anderson. You've grown three inches since last season." Wolf snorted inside me, and I willed my face to keep from coloring at his insinuation that he was that much more mature than me. He was scarcely a winter older, but he'd already been Alpha of his pack for three years after his father's unexpected death. I was still my father's Beta.

"It is good to see you, Richard." We clasped arms, though Wolf felt a shiver of unease as Richard's wide hand squeezed my forearm.

"It has been too long," Richard conceded.

The sharp ringing of a metal triangle made me wince and we turned to see Edith, Rebekkah's adopted human sister, standing on the porch.

"Robert says to set the tables for the feast," Edith called from the porch. Her eyes found the knot of Richard, Rebekkah, and me, and she quickly hung up the triangle on its peg and made her way towards the fire pit.

"Richard, Anderson, it's so good to see you both!" Younger than the three of us, Edith, too, had grown into a young woman.

Before anyone could respond, a strong, rich voice could be heard coming from just inside the big house.

"Here is your cane, Robert."

Wolf picked up the scent of tar, smoke, and fish as the front door opened. My eyes widened as I took in a tall warrior with long black braids coming over his bare shoulders. The tall man held the door and the click of a wooden staff on the planks echoed in the clearing.

"Ho, ho, who is this then?" Richard mumbled.

"That is Taly. He's the Beta of the Lenape," Rebekkah answered, her voice holding no emotion.

My eyebrows lifted. The Lenape were Native people to this area. Once our European packs had drifted over from the old world, we'd found brethren among their numbers. While not all the Lenape could shift at will the way our pack members could, certain members—particularly the chief's family—all carried the gene. Those among their tribe that could shift were held with great reverence. I didn't relish having to fight one as skilled as Taly was sure to be.

We all ate dinner together as twilight fell. After, my father helped Robert move to a stump covered in blankets so that he could address us. Rebekkah knelt beside her father, Edith on his other side.

Richard nudged me. "What do you make of Taly?" He jutted his chin towards the dark-haired man across the fire pit. Taly tapped tobacco into a long clay pipe.

"I've heard of him, but I've not formally met him before tonight. Rebekkah speaks well of the relationship between his tribe and her pack." Relations with the Lenape would be important, regardless of who inherited the Hawthorne pack.

Richard's brow furrowed. Before I could ask him his thoughts, Robert's weathered voice rose unsteadily over his pack and guests.

"I thank you all for coming," he began, his voice rusty. He coughed once into his handkerchief and Wolf caught the faintest tang of blood. My belly constricted. I'd always admired Robert Hawthorne. "As you all know, my time grows short. I have summoned you here for the ancient rituals—*Lacessere*. One of you," he paused to look at Richard, Taly, and me, "the winner of the Lacessere, will take over my position as Alpha of the Hawthorne pack." His eyes turned sorrowful as he gazed at his assembled pack. His pack was twelve strong, with a few cubs not yet old enough to shift to their wolf forms. And Edith.

"You will take Rebekkah as your mate, and in doing so,

take her pack and her lands to merge with your own. All that is mine will transfer to the winner once Rebekkah has accepted your Bite of Claimship."

Glancing at Rebekkah next to her father, I saw a light blush stain her cheeks in the dancing firelight. Wolf paced inside me.

Robert continued, "Three of the ancient rituals of Lacessere will be completed. Tomorrow each of you will fight to see who is the strongest among you. The weakest will be disqualified. The day after, there will be a race to see who is the swiftest and who finds the wisest course through the forest. Lastly, if needed, Rebekkah will bestow her favor. The wolf who finishes two of the three challenges victorious will be proclaimed Alpha." Robert's next cough ripped through the silent air.

"Papa," Edith worried, "let us get you back into the house where it is warm and dry. This night air cannot be good for your chest." Robert nodded tiredly at her.

"My thanks for your attendance, Richard, Anderson, Taly. I bid you all good eve. We will begin the rituals tomorrow once we break our fast." He rose stiffly, my father at his right arm, Edith at his left. "Rebekkah, please see to our guests' comfort," he said as he allowed Father to lead him back to his cabin.

Rebekkah blinked rapidly and I knew she held back her tears. I wanted to go to her, to hold her, but feared it would not be well received amidst our present company.

"Come with me, I'll show you where you all will stay the night." She turned away from the fire.

She led the three of us—the competitors for her pack, her lands, and her hand—behind her house to where three tents had been pitched. It was part of the ancient rituals—to spend the night solitarily before any challenge began.

"Sleep well, Richy...Richard, Anderson, Taly," she said quietly.

I squeezed her arm gently as she passed me, and then she was gone.

A makeshift ring was created with dyed rope strung between trees to mark off a large area for the fighting.

Richard's face was impassive, Taly's open but blank. I hoped my face didn't show the nerves jittering over my skin. My morning meal sat like stones in my gut.

Straws were drawn, and to my ashamed relief, Taly and Richard drew to fight first. I stood outside the ring, clenching my long straw, Rebekkah beside me, and her pack gathered around the perimeter.

Richard entered the ring first, his wolf huge and black like a panther. His swaggering gait left no doubt of his Alpha status. Taly came in opposite, also black, but sleek, trim, and shiny like a raven—lithe and quick. Richard's eyes narrowed as a growl rumbled deep in his chest.

"Fight fair, but fight hard," Robert called. And the match began.

Richard lunged with a snarl that set the hairs on the back of my neck standing straight up. He attacked Taly's smaller wolf with a ferocity that shook me. Beside me, Rebekkah gasped as Richard attempted to sink his teeth into Taly's neck. Her fingers wrapped around mine as her anxiety rippled through the tightness of her grip.

Nausea roiled through my belly. Wolf thrummed at the thought of a good fight while the rest of me battled my dread. I was a good fighter, but more than prowess was at stake. Rebekkah was at stake. I squeezed her fingers.

Taly yelped as Richard savagely clamped his teeth around his back leg. In a move that sent my heart racing to my throat, Taly whipped up on his front legs, his free back leg catching Richard across the muzzle.

Richard grunted in pain as Taly's claws caught the delicate skin of his nose and ripped a thin line up to his eye. Both were now bloodied.

With a great shake and a howl that rage made into a roar, Richard threw himself and his considerable weight against Taly, going for the smaller wolf's throat.

Gaping jaws locked against each other as the sounds of the fight lifted to the trees and sent the wildlife sprinting for cover.

Blood sprinkled the ground as the black wolves circled each other. Richard's eyes were frenzied, and Taly increasingly used his speed to hop and dance out of the way of Richard's glinting incisors. Rebekkah squeezed my hand, her face pale. Her fear was metallic in my nostrils. Even Wolf recoiled as he watched the inflicted savageness as the battle dragged on.

Richard lunged, his Alphaship rippling over his muscled form. Taly, lithe though he was, couldn't escape Richard's teeth.

Richard's teeth came down like daggers, catching Taly at the side of his neck.

Taly yelped as the teeth sunk in, piercing through the thick fur of his ruff. Richard clamped his jaws harder, giving Taly a solid shake. Blood dripped. Taly went limp, conceding. Richard didn't let go.

With another mighty shake, he flung Taly several feet away from him.

Rebekkah gasped as Richard threw back his head and howled victorious.

Wolf bristled. It may have been his right as the victor of the match, but his actions were arrogant. It set my teeth on edge.

My childhood friend would have cared more for his opponent's injuries. Richard had changed. He was more powerful, more aggressive. More ruthless.

Taly shifted back, his hand clamped around the dripping punctures in his neck. Rebekkah let go my hand and clasped her own together under her chin as she averted her eyes from Taly's nakedness.

Someone handed him a robe. He moved awkwardly, covered in blood and obviously in pain though his wounds were healing. Shock rooted me to the spot. I should have moved to help him, but thoughts of my own upcoming fight with Richard immobilized me. Wolf whined.

Taly cleared his throat and wiped some of the blood from his wound onto a rag. It smeared his already tanned skin to a deep red. The smack of blood filled the clearing.

Richard still stood proudly in his wolf's fur.

Taly turned to face him. "There is *piskakwihële* in you," he rasped. "Darkness." He turned to Robert, one long braid falling off his shoulder. "Robert. You are my friend and ally. But I will no longer be part of this. I withdraw myself from consideration."

"Taly," Robert began. A cough cut off his concern. Taly bowed and disappeared into the forest.

I battled only with Richard now. He was bigger and stronger than me.

And full of darkness?

Once lunch ended, Richard's wounds were fully healed, and it was time for my fight against him.

"You are smarter than he is," my father whispered as we stood at the edge of the clearing. He squeezed my shoulder. I swallowed hard. I glanced at Rebekkah. A word from her in my favor would boost my spirits. Instead, she sat next to Edith, clenching her sister's hand, and chewing the fingernails of her other. Her eyes stared at the ground, flitting to Richard once.

My stomach sank.

Wolf bolstered me, puffing out his chest. It did not matter if Rebekkah fancied Richard. She had agreed to marry the winner of the trials. I was capable. And I loved her. Surely in time, she could learn to love me, too?

If I won.

Richard circled the ring, the sun glinting off his black fur, waiting for me. I melted back into the woods and let my wolf come forth. My bones creaked and popped, sinews stretching, muscles cording, fur sprouting to cover me in a silver casing. I shook my head, feeling the glorious ripples of wind over my fur and inhaled deeply. Deep loam and fresh buds met my nose. And the lingering coppery scent of the bloodshed in the ring this morning.

Wolf growled low in our throat. That would not be our fate.

"Fight fair, and fight hard," Robert said.

The match began.

Richard didn't lunge for me as he had at Taly. Wolf crouched low to the ground. I'd watched Richard's form earlier in the day. He'd taken a different approach for me. We'd often fought to hone our skills when we were early teenagers. But never had so much weighed on the outcome.

A branch crackled under Richard's paw.

Like a streak of lightning I darted towards him, catching his tail and giving it a sharp bite before letting go and moving back.

Richard swung around and nearly clipped my flank as I spun just out of reach. He growled low in his throat. He knew I tried to provoke him. Richard got careless when his anger took over.

He sprung up high in the air and I scarcely had time to move before he pounced. His front claws raked down my ribs, opening my flesh. I winced but locked my teeth around the mouthful of his chest. I got mostly fur and had to let go before Richard twisted free and bit down on my neck. Wolf tasted blood and I knew I'd opened a small wound on him.

We were both bleeding as we circled. Wolf felt the energy coursing through us. As if set off by some internal trigger, Richard and I lunged at each other at the same time, teeth gnashing, paws whipping.

Snarls and grunts bashed together as our feet churned the dust, covering us in a cloud of dirt and blood as our teeth increasingly found purchase.

Retreating to our sides again, once more we circled. Richard's nostrils flared. Wolf growled at the challenge, ignoring the myriad of little nicks we'd sustained. Richard was ready to end this fight.

He lunged again and this time, I swerved to the side, biting at his flanks, but missing as he moved at the last moment. With a twist and his full weight behind it, Richard pinned me to the ground. I struggled, but with his considerable extra weight, I was stuck. I did the only thing I could, I exposed my neck in order to reach up and bite his.

I caught his throat, and for a moment, Richard stilled, knowing I had him. With one last vicious snarl, Richard ripped his head away from me, opening his own neck as he pulled away from my teeth.

Blood streamed into my eyes as I tried to roll away, but Richard, still on top, bit down on the back of my neck. He had my ruff, but he had muscle, too. And he clamped his jaws. His teeth pierced my hide and Wolf barked.

I couldn't twist free. Richard's mouth had the whole upper part of my neck in his mouth. He growled menacingly and shook. Clenched in his jaws, my head and neck flung helplessly.

I could not free myself. Richard won the fight.

CHAPTER 2

Rebekkah

I winced as Pa coughed wetly in his room down the hall. Edith raised sympathetic eyes to mine, her chin quivering. It wouldn't be long. Probably days, weeks at most.

Crossing our shared room, I tucked my adopted sister under my arm and squeezed her shoulders. When we'd found her as a baby beside a burned-out wagon on the outskirts of our territory, we'd brought her home and she'd been raised alongside me.

"I always hoped Pa would be the one to change me when I turned sixteen," Edith whispered. It was illegal in our pack to change someone before they'd reached the age of majority. Edith turned sixteen in four months.

"I wish he could, too. We've waited years to be wolves together." I smoothed her hair back from her forehead. "But our new Alpha will surely change you still. I will ensure it's a condition of the inheritance."

Edith's shoulders relaxed a fraction. "Truly? You'll speak with Richy and Ander?"

I nodded, swallowing past the lump in my throat. Of all I stood to lose and gain, having my sister with me in the months ahead was the one constant I counted on.

"Who do you want to win, Rebekkah?" Edith's whispered question drove ice into my stomach. Even being honest with myself, I wasn't sure.

"I want what's best for the pack," I hedged. "Richy has already had years of experience leading his own pack. He's strong. He's a fighter. He could defend the pack and lead with purpose." I paused, thinking of the way he'd shaken Taly by the scruff today. I felt a frown creep over my forehead. "Ander has always understood *me* better, though I think I've always fancied Richy. I need the man who will best understand our pack."

"Rebekkah, you've longed for Richard Woods to show interest in you since you were thirteen." Edith teased with a poke to my ribs.

My frown shifted into a chagrined smile. "That is true. But now that the choice is staring me in the face, I'm not sure who would make the best leader. Richard may be able to lead the pack better, and I have always been somewhat romantically interested in him...but Anderson has changed. He's got this quiet way about him, this silent strength."

"You think he'd be a better mate?" Edith's question gave voice to my internal thoughts.

"Maybe. But I must think of the pack first," I reminded myself as much as Edith. "If Richard wins the race tomorrow, it will not matter. The need for my favor will be nullified."

"I hope you have the choice."

"Part of me hopes the choice remains with me, but the other part of me wishes Pa would make the choice. Wolf is as confused as the rest of me," I confessed. She paced within me, excited and anxious as the human half of me.

Edith squeezed my hand and helped me turn down the blanket on the bed.

I swallowed again, thinking that tomorrow night I'd be sharing a bed with someone else.

My blood chilled.

"Are you scared? About the Claiming? And...the rest?" Edith seemed to read my thoughts again.

"Not until this moment." This would be the last night I'd share this room with my sister. Tomorrow I'd move into the smaller cabin with my mate—my husband, and future Alpha of the Hawthorne pack.

"Will you let him Claim you publicly?" Edith slid under the covers, shivering.

"It's part of the ritual," I said. Wolf squirmed inside. Claiming was intimate. I rubbed my nose where the bite would go—gently closing over my muzzle. It wasn't something I wanted to share with the entire pack, only with my intended, but the ritual decreed that the Bite of Claimship be done publicly so that everyone might see the transfer of power through my bloodline to the next chosen Alpha.

"Maybe you can spend some time with Richy and Ander separately tomorrow morning before the race. Get to know them again before you have to make your decision," Edith suggested.

"If the decision remains with me." I blew out the candle and crept into bed, though my mind turned things over and over. Richard. Anderson. Alpha. My Hawthorne blood. Sleep did not come quickly.

Dawn broke over the horizon in reds and oranges that spilled liquid gold onto the treetops and set the mist rising from the forest like ethereal fingers weaving their way to the skies.

Pa's handkerchief was spotted with blood when I went to help him that morning. Blood dotted his pillow.

Wolf howled inside me. I loved my papa so.

He put a heavy hand on my shoulder. "Be brave, my sweet, wild girl. The pack and your new husband will need you." He squeezed once and then let me help him to his feet.

I put on a bright face as I exited the cabin a few minutes later, my hair swinging in a simple plait down my back. I cinched my shawl closer as the brisk spring wind blew its chilly breath over me.

Wolf nudged me when I saw Anderson crouched next to the communal fire pit coaxing the flames to life. He readied things so the pack could eat together—what I'd come outside to do. Something warmed inside me at his thoughtfulness.

"Good morning, Rebekkah," he said quietly in the silence of the morning. No one else was about yet. I always rose early to tend the morning fire.

"Morning, Ander." The nickname slipped out after talking with Edith last night. I colored slightly, wondering if he'd mind the way Richard had. He smiled softly.

"Come sit. I've got the chickory tea finished."

"You *have* been awake some time," I said, surprised and pleased.

I sat on a log near him and watched as he deftly poured me a steaming cup of liquid. Our fingers brushed as he handed me the cup. Glancing up, his eyes were open, kind.

"Your pa have a rough night, or are you...anxious about today?"

My eyebrows lifted. "A bit of both, if I'm honest, I suppose." He sat next to me on the log, closer than he needed to. Our knees brushed. I wouldn't have noticed this time last year, but now it seemed significant. I didn't pull away.

"Is there anything I can do, Rebekkah?" His deep voice dipped even lower as he said my name and sent tingles rushing to my toes.

I shook my head and took a sip of the steaming brew.

"Mm, did you put sugar in this?" Sugar was costly.

He smiled shyly. "I brought some with me. Picked it up in town before winter and was saving it. I know how much you like sweet things."

Heat curled inside me. "Thank you, Ander. For coming. For fighting. For bringing me sugar." I smiled and knew it reached my eyes. Anderson was not the strongest fighter. Yesterday had proved that. But he had other qualities that might make him a good leader. My smile faltered. Anderson would make a good mate.

"Are you nervous? About the race?" I asked him.

He took a sip from his own tin cup, staring at the dancing flames as he swallowed.

"Some. If I'm honest, I suppose." He repeated my words. "Richard is fast, but so am I. Neither of us has been here in a year, so neither of us will know how the forest has changed."

Silence fell between us, both unsure what to say next. We sipped our chickory tea together in the stillness.

CHAPTER 3

Richard

I forced my hackles to smooth back down when I saw Anderson and Rebekkah sitting so close to each other on the log near the fire pit. Wolf already felt protective of Rebekkah. She would be our mate.

Rebekkah's beauty was undeniable with her long dark hair, her big doe eyes brown like maple syrup, and her woman's figure that had my eyes lingering longer than was proper. And she'd been enamored with me since we were children. She'd be a good mate. I'd make sure she was content and well protected.

I was an Alpha. I had the experience she needed. I was who she wanted. And I didn't dare tell her how badly I needed her numbers. Sickness had decimated my pack last year. There were five of us left. We needed others. Wolves needed each other for protection. We couldn't easily live among the general populace, and life had been hard enough to hack out of the wilderness as a pack of eleven. I would not give up my status as Alpha and become subordinate by joining another pack, but if I won, then all the Hawthorne pack would assimilate under me. And I'd be sole holder of extensive lands. The woods would literally belong to the Woods pack. The thought sent a tingle of anticipation through my belly.

Wolf let out the faintest of growls as Rebekkah smiled down at her steaming cup and said something to Anderson. They were just far enough away that I couldn't eavesdrop, even with my sensitive wolf ears. They fell silent just as I stepped closer to listen. My fingers twitched in frustration.

Anderson saw me first and saluted me with his tin cup held in the air.

"Morning, Richard," he called.

"Anderson, Rebekkah. Rebekkah, would you take a short walk with me?" I offered my arm as I reached them.

"Of course." She took one more drink from her own tin cup, her eyes closing as she relished the taste. "Mm. It's delicious, Ander. Here. Save the rest of that. I want to savor it when I get back." She handed him the half-full cup of coffee. Anderson smiled and put it on the ground near the still-steaming pot. Wolf bristled, feeling like we'd been left out of something.

He quieted when Rebekkah took my proffered arm. I snuck a look back at Anderson to see his reaction. Seeing his fallen expression was not as gratifying as I expected.

I led us a short way into the woods into a patch of sun-dappled grass. The dew sparkled in the early sunshine and the river swished softly as it lapped against the rocky shoreline some ways down the hill.

"It's been a chilly spring," Rebekkah commented as she pulled her shawl tighter with one hand, leaving her other on my arm. Feeling confident, I moved and let her fingers slide through mine, twining our hands together.

My confidence faltered momentarily as I saw Rebekkah's raised eyebrow as she looked at our hands.

"What are you about, Richard?" she said.

"I just wanted to tell you how much this means to me. And how sorry I am about your father," I added.

"Thank you." Tears quickly rimmed her eyes and I wished I hadn't brought it up.

"You're more beautiful than last I saw you." It was true, not mere flattery.

She smiled, blinking her tears back. "You're still handsome as ever," she said softly. Wolf gloated inwardly.

I looked down at her; her face turned away. Gently, I put two fingers under her chin and raised her face, so we looked into each other's eyes.

Seeing her surprise brought a faint smile to my lips. I held her gaze a moment, letting her feel my dominance, my strength as an Alpha, before glancing at her lips and slowly lowering my head to hers.

"Richard?" she gasped as she stepped back, leaving my fingers cold in her absence.

"Rebekkah," I started, surprised she'd backed away. "You've wanted me to kiss you since we were children." I couldn't understand why she wouldn't let me kiss her now, since I was the obvious winner and had every intention of being her wedded mate by evening.

"Be that as it may," she stuttered, "if you win, then tonight you may kiss me as much as you like. But you haven't won just yet, and I'll keep my first kiss until then."

Leaving me dumbfounded and more than a little irked in the clearing, with a swirl of skirts, she returned to her pack. My pack. It would soon be my pack. My teeth grit together.

I was still in a foul mood when it came time to race. Wolf and I had both taken Rebekkah's rebuff personally. I didn't understand it. Didn't understand *her*. I'd been polite and charming to the rest of her pack that morning, polite to both her and Anderson, but inside I seethed. I *needed* her pack. I *wanted* her. And knew she wanted me. *Soon enough*, I told myself, letting my mind stray to thoughts of kissing her as much as I liked.

My anger fueled my desire to win. I emerged from the woods where I'd shifted and stood at the designated spot between two trees. Robert leaned against Lemuel Wolfe to the side. Anderson's silver wolf walked slowly up behind his father, touching his nose to Lemuel's shoulder in passing.

"Good luck, Son," Lemuel said softly. Robert wheezed into his handkerchief. I forced myself not to recoil as the sound brought memories of my dead pack surging through my mind.

Anderson trotted up beside me, politely giving me a customary scenting. I returned the gesture and got annoyed all over again when I caught a whiff of coffee laid over his normal pine and loam smell.

Rebekkah waited opposite her father, a red kerchief in her hand that she'd drop to signal the start of the race. I absently wondered where Edith was. She and Rebekkah had been practically sewn together at the side since my arrival. No matter. I had but to win this race, and my life would be set to rights, and my pack saved.

CHAPTER 4

Anderson

Wolf nearly frothed at the mouth with nerves. Richard's wolf stood next to us, huge, domineering, heavily muscled, and reeking of power. I shook my head, a light breeze catching the sensitive hairs on my ears. I was not subject to Richard. He was not my Alpha. I would lead my own pack someday—be my *own* Alpha. My father had seen to my instruction. I knew I had his confidence and his support. It lifted my spirits, knowing my father was behind me. I was sorry Richard could no longer have his father who had died several winters ago. But that was the reason he was Alpha now—and my stiffer competition because of it.

"Remember, it's not only who finishes first, but who finishes by finding the wisest course through the forest," Robert said. I was uncertain what he meant but I didn't think Richard knew either. All part of the ambiguity of Lacessere. "You must retrieve a branch from the Juniper tree under which Rebekkah was christened." I knew that tree. The three of us had played under its boughs many times as children. It was on the far side of the forest. "May you have strength, wisdom, and courage. Let no folly deter you." Robert finished.

My muscles tensed, bunched and ready to spring forward. I glanced at Rebekkah and felt a surge of heat when she met my gaze. My gaze—not Richard's—as she held the kerchief above her head.

"Go," she whispered as the red fabric fluttered in the breeze.

Richard and I were off like two fired musket rounds. We dodged, we wove, we dashed, claws tearing into the leafy topsoil.

The forest floor wasn't completely overgrown this early in the season though tender shoots and tiny vines snaked across the path as we thundered heedlessly over them, tearing up the dirt behind us.

Wolf ran for all he was worth. I mapped out the route I'd take in my head as my paws churned another spray of dirt behind me. Richard sprinted a few trees over, parallel to my course. I knew I could get to the juniper first if I took the short cut by the cave, but that would take me close to the bank of the river, and that could be a dangerous route if the path had crumbled at all.

What would the wisest course of action be? I saw Richard veer off to the left and knew he was going to take to the meadow. It was slightly longer in distance but easier running. His longer legs would have the advantage there if I followed.

Having no other choice if I wanted to win, I took the gamble and headed towards the short cut.

The spring had been cool, but mild, and luck shined on me as I galloped down the old deer trail. The path above the river was solid and I ate up the ground like fire licking up dry kindling.

Within minutes, my sides heaving, my tongue lolling, I came to the base of the hill that led up to Rebekkah's tree. Taking a quick scent as my feet propelled me upwards, I knew I'd beat Richard to the target. Panting, I let the spicy scent of juniper—the smell that always reminded me of Rebekkah—envelope me. Lunging up on my back paws, I tore a small branch. The sap was bitter and tangy as the end of the twig hit my lips. Ignoring the tingling it sent down my tongue, I gripped it in my teeth and set off back down the hill.

Richard howled as he saw me dashing down the hill. For a moment I thought he might come after me instead of the tree, but he kept to his course.

Fire raced through me. If I could keep my pace, I would beat Richard. I'd have earned my point and if Rebekkah chose me, she'd be my wife. My heart thundered as I urged Wolf faster.

A scream pierced the air and brought me up short. Again, shrilling pierced through the stillness of the woods.

Edith.

Without another thought to the race, I turned to find her. I yipped through my teeth, still clutching the juniper twig.

No answer. Fear snaked through my veins and I put my nose to the ground to find her scent. Richard rushed past me. My heart plummeted. *Let no folly deter you*, Robert had said. Surely, they'd let us redo the race. Edith was in trouble. Edith was no folly. I barked hard at Richard to help me find her. He ignored me. He ran so close past me that the wind off his wake blew my whiskers.

I yipped again for Edith, dropping my juniper twig.

Another cry, fainter, but clearly to the right. The wind changed directions and I caught her scent.

Barreling after it, I caught a glimpse of her pale purple dress, crumpled by the side of the river path I'd come on.

"Anderson!" she gasped as she saw my head. I barked, assessing her as I came up next to her.

"I've twisted my ankle." She pointed and I noted her face was blotchy. She was scared. Yipping again, I nudged my head under her arm and indicated she should climb up on my back. It was awkward, and there was more fur pulling than I cared for, but in the end, she was on my back, her hands secured around my neck.

"Run fast, Anderson," she whispered. "I've got a sprig of the tree in my pocket. We may be able to catch Richard yet."

I sighed, knowing Richard had won, but still hopeful that they'd let us redo the race since it was for Edith and her well-being that I'd left the course. At Edith's insistence, I still hurried. It was slower going carrying her, even though she was slight. I was glad it was spring and not full summer with leafy branches that would have scratched at her as we made our way back to the pack.

Richard was strutting around, fully dressed in his trousers and shirt, having had time to change completely by the time Edith and I made it back into the clearing. My heart sank to my toes. Richard must have told them what happened—that I went after Edith. Would they not allow the race to be redone? Had I lost Rebekkah forever? Wolf wanted to howl, but I held it in. I could not give way to my grief so publicly.

CHAPTER 5

Rebekkah

"Edith!" I gasped, seeing Anderson trot into the clearing
with my sister on his back.

"I'm all right. I just twisted my ankle on a loose stone by
the river," she said. Pa looked at her with concern from his
seat against a tree.

I hurried to them and helped her slide off Anderson.
Unable to help myself and to let him know my apprecia-
tion, I let my fingers run over the silky fur of his shoulder.

His head came up and his blue eyes fixed on me. I patted him once more and then looped an arm around Edith's waist as she put hers around my shoulders. I helped her hobble over to Pa.

Mr. Wolfe brought clothes for his son. Quickly he stepped behind a few trees and emerged shortly after, rumpled, but dressed.

"Edith, are you well? I hope it wasn't too rough coming back." His first concern was for Edith. My heart swelled with gratitude.

"I will be fine. It just needs a compress and some time. Thank you for coming to my aide." Edith's cheeks flushed.

Anderson nodded, relieved. "Mr. Hawthorne, surely we might be able to complete the race again tomorrow?"

"I am sorry, Anderson, but this race was final," Pa said, light dancing in his eyes.

"He did say to let nothing deter us," Richard offered as he came next to Anderson, clapping a sympathetic hand to Anderson's shoulder. My heart squeezed painfully in my chest.

"Anderson, did you retrieve a twig of the juniper tree?" Pa asked.

"It's right here," Edith said and supplied a twig from her dress pocket.

"Richard, it is true you finished the race first. You retrieved a branch from Rebekkah's christening tree, and you let nothing deter you," Pa said.

Richard stood a little straighter, and my palms began to sweat.

"I have won two of the three ritual challenges," Richard said, pride in his voice. I suddenly felt faint. "I claim my—"

"Not so quickly," Pa interrupted but stopped to cough. Richard's eyes narrowed. Pa wiped his lips with his handkerchief, wadding it up quickly so no one would see the blood, though we could all smell it. My heart stuttered painfully against my breastbone as Pa continued. "While you did complete the challenge quickest, you did not find the wisest course through the forest. When you heard Edith cry out, were you not distressed for her safety? I said let no *folly* deter you. Surely my daughter is no mere folly?"

Richard's jaw locked and fire practically shot from his eyes. Blood pounded in my ears.

"Anderson, knowing he might lose the race, went after her, putting her safety above his own desires. That is wisdom. The victory of this challenge goes to Anderson."

Thunder crossed Richard's face as Anderson sucked in a breath. Blood rushed to my head, and I swayed.

"You have tricked me, old man. I will not forget this." Richard glared at Pa.

Pa inclined his head to him. "It was a part of the challenge, though you were not supposed to injure yourself," Pa said to Edith. My heart hammered. They had planned this? "We will meet again in two hours. Rebekkah will give her favor to one of you, and she will receive his Claiming Bite. Reverend Heatherford will join us and will marry you this eve.

I sat in front of my dressing table staring at my wavy reflection in the mirror. Absently, I brushed my hair. It was already shining, but the motion calmed my racing heart.

My choice. The fate of the pack rested on my shoulders. I was both elated and terrified that I would choose my own mate.

But how did I choose between my two best friends? One a strong, dominant leader who could protect the pack, the other thoughtful, caring, who understood me.

Anderson was by no means weak, but would he grow into that dominant leader that Richard was already? Richard, who I'd been infatuated with since I was a girl, who made my blood race, and Anderson, my solemn, dependable friend.

Wolf nudged me. I knew who I wanted.

Determination shone from my eyes and reflected in the mirror. A knock sounded at the door and I scented Edith's floral overtones. She'd put on rose water.

"Come," I said softly.

Edith cracked the door and hobbled in with the makeshift cane Mr. Wolfe had quickly fashioned for her.

"May I help you dress your hair?" She smiled shyly.

I smiled. "Of course. Here. Sit on the bed and I'll move my stool to sit in front of you."

"You've decided, haven't you? You seem at peace." Her eyes searched my face.

"Far from at peace, but yes. I've made my choice." She didn't prod me further, knowing it would be unfair of me to tell her before the decision was made formally. Her nimble fingers braided up sections of my hair, twisting and pinning it into an intricate coil that laced my head like a crown.

"One more thing," she said as she pointed to the vase of white snow drops on my dresser. I smiled and handed them to her. "There. Now you truly look like a woman about to wed. the flowers are the perfect touch against your dark hair." Edith smiled as she took in her handywork. I looked once more in the mirror.

"You've made me beautiful, Edith."

"You are beautiful all by yourself."

I hugged her tightly. "I shall miss you," I whispered.

"Don't be a silly goose. You'll only be moving a few paces away into a new house. We'll still see each other every day."

"I suppose you're right."

The sun seemed to set the trees on fire as it began its
descent behind the far hills. A tremor shook my hands
and I clasped them together against the blue of my skirt.
I wore my mother's wedding dress and it filled me with a
bittersweet pang. She'd passed many winters ago, though I
desperately wished she could be here with me today. Edith
clumped down the steps behind me and followed a few
paces behind.

Richard and Anderson were both freshly washed and
groomed. My eyes flitted over them both, my decision
knotting my stomach. Wolf nudged me, reassuring me that
we'd made the right choice. Richard was confident and
straight, Anderson hopeful and solid.

My pack gathered around us in a semi-circle. The trees
blew in the fragrance of the fading day and drifted around
me, blowing my skirts and teasing tendrils of hair that
Edith had left loose at my temples. I stopped a few paces
in front of the waiting people, Edith not far to my right,
offering her silent support as Pa looked on with Mr. Wolfe
and the minister at his side. Reverend Heatherford was a
preacher from a neighboring pack with no eligible Alphas
or Betas. Pa trusted him. I swallowed. He'd marry me within the hour.

I looked at Richard and then at Anderson. I cleared my throat and looked once more to Pa. He smiled and nodded his head. He was entrusting the future of the pack to me. It was both a great gift and a great burden. Wolf nudged us, and I took a breath and stood up straighter.

"Thank you both, Richard, Anderson. Your willingness to come and make a bid for me, for my pack, is felt deeply. But, as we all know, I may only choose one of you." I swallowed again as my heart pounded and my voice shook. "I choose Anderson Wolfe."

There was a loud snarl, and then several things happened at once.

I watched in horror as time slowed. Richard's wolf ripped from his skin. Understanding dawned and I realized he was going to force his Claiming Bite on me, taking me, the pack, my lands, as his own against my will.

Before I had time to scream, to shift, to breathe, Anderson's silver wolf bounded between me and a lunging Richard.

With a mighty sweep of his front paw, Anderson smacked Richard's mouth away. Anderson turned, and a sharp stab of pain shot up my arm as Anderson's teeth sank into my hand. Dizziness consumed me as Wolf reacted.

We'd been Claimed. By Anderson. On the hand. Relief and fear thrummed through me. I had no time to process further as Richard threw back his head and gave an angry howl that sent the hairs on the back of my neck straight up. Wolf lurched inside me. Richard's wolf looked me in the eye, Wolf squirming under his baleful gaze.

Anderson was in front of me, lips pulled back in a menacing growl, every hair bristled in possessiveness.

Wolves shifted around us as my pack quickly came to my defense. Sounds of ripping, pattering clothing, and angry barks filled the clearing.

In the midst of the shifting and confusion, Richard did the one thing he knew would hurt me most.

He lunged at Edith, his teeth sinking into her neck. She screamed. I screamed. My own screams turned to wracking sobs as Edith convulsed, her gown splitting open as her limbs transformed. Fur poked through her skin and her eyes rolled back into her head and tufted ears poked out her skull. Her body morphed, twisting, snapping, her keening howls filling the air as sobs wracked my chest. In mere moments, she lay on the ground, a wolf. Changed and Claimed by Richard. She was now part of his pack—shackled to him and forever gone from me. My heart ached and Wolf howled inside me.

Anderson's flank touched me as he kept his body between me and Richard. Anderson howled, understanding on a base level that part of his pack had been stolen.

Richard shifted back to his human skin but stayed crouched over Edith.

"I have taken from you what would have remained yours if you'd chosen me—the rightful winner. Now you will be without the one you love forever. She is mine now. And every time you think of your loss, you'll know your mistake." Hatred made his words deathly low, like a fissure opening in the depths.

"Edith," I whispered as her wolf turned anguished eyes to me. She pointed her nose to the sky and howled, but it was cut short as her face began changing shape once more. Her mouth opened in silent agony her cries cut short as her body shifted to skin once more. Without waiting for another moment, Richard scooped her up in his arms and ran into the woods. Anderson moved to go after him. I placed my hand on his shoulder.

"It's done," I choked. Edith was lost to me. Even if we went after her and brought her back, short of killing

Richard, she'd be bound to him for her entire life. Such was the pull of the bite of the werewolf over a human.

The minister married me under a veil of tears. What should have been a happy moment of rejoicing was a moment of subdued sorrow. Anderson and I pledged ourselves to each other and to our pack. But Edith was gone, and so was a piece of my heart. Tears tracked down Pa's weathered face.

"I'm so sorry, my sweet daughter," he whispered as he hugged me tight after I was properly Mrs. Wolfe. The Hawthorne name would end with me.

Anderson held me that night. Alone in our house, sitting on our bed, I let my tears fall.

"I wish there was something I could do," he murmured against my hair, his hands wrapped around me like a cocoon. I took a shuddering breath and felt the steady beating of his heart beneath my damp cheek.

"I'm so sorry that choosing me has brought you so much pain." His quiet words dropped into the blackness of our room. Eyebrows lifting, Wolf pricked her ears forward. Searching his face in the shadows, I recognized the burden of guilt he carried.

Pulling back, I struggled to sit up, still nestled in his lap, but able to make out his face in the dark with my wolf's enhanced sight.

I took a shuddering breath. "Anderson, Richard's doing is not your fault." I tentatively put my hand against his cheek, feeling the rough stubble along his jaw. "If anything, it only confirmed that I made the wiser choice. No." I shook my head. "This sorrow has nothing to do with you. It's entirely Richard's doing." We were quiet a moment, Ander leaning into my hand. Slowly the backs of his fingers combed my hair behind my ear and trailed softly to the back of my neck, cradling my face. His thumb skimmed my chin.

"Rebekkah, do you know how long I've wanted to marry you?"

"No," I said, genuinely surprised.

"Probably as long as you wanted Richard to be your mate. Why did you choose me instead of him? You've always fancied him." There was no condemnation, only curiosity in his voice. His thumb brushed my chin again. Wolf nudged me as budding awareness tingled in my belly.

"Richard is many things. Was many good things. And I *have* always fancied him. But you have always understood me. You take care of people. Richard is a fighter. You seek peace first, but you're not afraid to fight. And you chose to go after Edith." My voice wobbled. "Today I realized that my fancy of Richard is a girlish thing, and I'm a girl no more. I need *you*. I *wanted you* for my mate. Not Richard. You will be the leader the pack needs. The one who will care for them and love them. Love me," I finished so softly I wondered if he heard.

He stroked a piece of hair behind my ear. "I will always love you, Rebekkah."

Wolf thrummed in my chest and heat slid through me to my toes.

"I will love you, too, Ander."

And then I kissed him.

Carefully, I plucked the last of the wildflowers that grew beside the path. The wind whistled, sharp with just a hint of the coming autumn chill. My hand slid to the soft swell of my belly where a new life grew. If it was a boy, we'd name him Robert after my Pa, Edith if it was a girl. The middle name would be Hawthorne.

With a sigh, I sank to my knees in front of the simple stone carved in plain letters, *Robert Samuel Hawthorne*. I gently laid the bright blossoms across his grave.

"He'd be proud of you," Ander said quietly beside me.

I knew in my heart that Anderson was right.

Part II

Chapter 6

Edith

Anger, sorrow, loss, pain, all rippled over me in dizzying anguish. Calling out, my voice cracked as agony ripped over my scalp, shattered my back, and held my limbs rigid. Thrashing against the man who carried me, I was lost again to the wolf.

Sobs wracked my chest as fur sliced through my tender skin, burning and tearing. Terror clouded everything else, even as scents of the forest I loved blasted into my nostrils with a force previously unknown to me. Overwhelmed and heartbroken, a whimper escaped my lips as they morphed into my wolf's muzzle.

I'd always wanted to be a werewolf. But never like this. Instead of being tied to the people I loved, instead, the creature I was becoming drew mental ties, hard and unbreakable, to *him*.

"Peace, Edith. We'll stop momentarily." Richard. The man I was bound to with indestructible ties, the man I both loathed and loved.

Though I'd never told my sister, I had always harbored a deep well of affection for both Richard and Anderson—Richard especially. The deep spring of that affection was now utterly dry—tainted by deceit and grief. I had been used and betrayed in the most unthinkable manner imaginable. Cut off from everyone and everything I knew.

Had I not suffered enough tragedy in my young life?

Moments later, the shift began again, and I screamed with the intensity. Bones crunched, muscles twisted, fur sliced back through my skin, pink and naked in the moonlight. Sweat broke out over my body, and shivers tore through me, adding to my misery.

"Here, Edith. Here," Richard said softly. Gently he laid my aching body on the grass beside the river. I shivered uncontrollably, likely from shock as much as the spring chill. "I'm sorry, Edith," Richard mumbled. "What have I done?"

I turned my face from him, curling in on myself, tears leaking from the edges of my eyes. Squeezing them shut, I tried to block him out, block out everything, focusing only on breathing in and out, intent only on surviving this moment to the next. The wolf inside me moved, whining in sympathy. Letting my senses focus on her, she nudged me. We were one. Though still encased in my human form, Wolf tipped back her head and howled, angry at our circumstances, but filled with joy at her creation.

Wheezing escaped my lips, the human manifestation of my internal struggle. I sobbed in earnest as my chest constricted and my heart broke all over again. I hated Richard for what he'd done to me. Hated that he'd stolen my family, hated that he'd cheated me of what my heart had desired—joining my father's pack—and defiled my desire to become a werewolf by giving me this version of it that bound me to him. Hated that I'd once loved him.

"Edith, can you speak?" Richard knelt, devoid of clothing himself, at my back.

"I have nothing to say to you," I rasped, trying to cover myself with my arms. More tears fell as he gently put his hand on my bare shoulder.

"Edith, I'm sorry. I have wronged you grievously in my anger and desperation."

I could hear how much those words cost him to say. Richard, the proud Alpha who had wanted my sister. Wolf stirred within me. In a sudden flurry of rage, Wolf erupted. Turning in my wolf's body, I lashed out with my teeth, biting Richard hard across his forearm. Blood welled in my mouth, waking a dark place inside me that hungered for more. Releasing him, I backed away, whimpering as Richard's blood dripped down my chin.

"Edith," he gasped. I froze, coils of emotion wrapping around and squeezing—ties like a rope being stretched between the two of us, binding me ever more tightly to Richard. "You...you've Claimed me." Richard stared at me, jaw slack, as the full horror of what I'd just done descended on me. In my anger, I'd completed what Richard had started. He'd changed me and forced me to be a part of his pack, lashing me to him. But what I'd just done had bound *him* to *me*. Unwittingly though the act was done, we were Claimed.

Chapter 7

Richard

The evil I'd done to Edith curdled in my belly, even as Claimship overtook me, igniting places inside me long-thought dead. In wonder, I stared at Edith's wolf eyes—yellow in the pale moonlight. *Mate*. A surge of protectiveness filled me, only adding to the confusion of emotions already aroused and clashing in my chest.

I hadn't meant to hurt Edith—I'd only wanted to cause Rebekkah pain. She'd robbed me of what I needed most to survive—I *needed* her pack. I *wanted* Rebekkah. Had wanted her. Wolf assured me now that I only wanted Edith, though the feeling didn't sit naturally. Stealing Edith from Rebekkah had surely caused her heart the agony I'd felt when Anderson had won the Lacessere. In my recklessness, I'd ripped Edith from her home. I hadn't thought of her at all. Only of my anger. My pride. My pack. Maintaining my place as Alpha.

But all my pride and anger were stripped from me now as I hunched on the grass, looking at Edith—my mate.

"Edith. We *are*." My voice cracked.

"How could you?" she whispered brokenly, back in her skin.

Shame rose in the back of my throat, and I stared at the ground. "I needed your pack. Mine is dying." The words shoved themselves from my mouth.

Her quick intake of breath brought my gaze back to her face.

"What do you mean your pack is dying? What have you forced me into?"

"Consumption. We—I couldn't save them. The entire pack. Only a few of us survived. Not even our werewolf genes could fight it off."

Edith's hatred gentled. "Why did you not ask for help?"

Pride prickled the back of my neck. "I do not beg."

"Perhaps you should have. If you had, we would have helped you." The ice in her voice drove my guilt deeper. "And I'd not be bound to you now."

My eyes shut at the pain in her voice before my own anger whispered to the surfaced again.

"I am bound to you now, too." I met her gaze. Wolf shook out his coat inside. I was still the Alpha. "You are my mate now." The words came through gritted teeth. Some of my ire ebbed as tears welled in her eyes and her expression turned utterly lost. "You will always have a place of esteem within the pack. You are mine."

"I don't want to be yours. I am going home. I can still break ties to you and go home."

Panic punched me in the chest. *Mate!* Wolf bashed against me as my pride and anger kindled. I would not lose my mate to the pack that abandoned me, tricked me, and denied what I had rightfully won. Alpha swelled in my chest. "You will not return to the Hawthorne or Wolfe packs ever again. *I forbid it.* You are of the Woods now. You belong to *me.*"

Whimpering, she scampered back from me on all fours, horror and terror stamped on every one of her features as my Alpha command settled onto her. My gut twisted.

"What more can you take from me? You've turned me against my will, taken me from my home. I'll never see my sister again and never tell my pa how much I love him or tell him goodbye." Tears streaked her cheeks as she drew a shuddering breath.

I sighed, pained, but justified in ordering her to remain with me. I couldn't let her go back. I couldn't be so weak. She was my *mate*. We were bound to each other. Looking back to her, sadness twinged in my middle as anger and fear scrawled across her features.

Moonlight sifted from the treetops onto her bare skin that I only now realized was naked. Unease gathered in my belly. I swallowed and yanked my eyes back to her face.

A terrified squeak escaped her lips as she hurriedly tried to cover herself with her arms.

"Easy, Edith. I'm no monster," I tried to reassure her, my eyes carefully trained on her face.

She barked a harsh laugh, and I shoved the guilt that threatened to surface back into the dark recesses where I couldn't sense it.

"Come. Let us rejoin our pack. It's still cold out, and the pack depends upon me. I cannot abandon them, and if we catch our death here, we help no one. Can you shift to your fur?"

She shook her head, still huddled in a ball.

"I will command you to shift." I held out my hands, trying to placate her. "I don't want to force you to do anything...else," I added for good measure, "but we need to keep moving."

CHAPTER 8

Edith

Blank eyes, dull, lifeless, gaunt, barely among the living, the remains of the Woods pack gathered to greet their Alpha and his new wife. Wolf whined inside me. These people *did* depend on Richard. Two men, one child too young yet to shift. What desolation the sickness had wreaked.

Glancing at Richard's face as we paced into the village, it was plain, even on his wolf's features, how much he cared and worried over his pack. A few yips sounded from a mangy wolf that rounded a cabin at our arrival, but mostly, the three in skin—even the child—moved like old men bent by the cares of the world to come greet us.

A bony woman exited a small cabin carrying a bundle of clothes with her.

For us. We'll change and introduce you in skin, Richard said through our newly-established mate link. The woman dipped her head and placed the clothing on the ground. Richard scooped them up in his mouth and nudged me towards the largest of the log houses.

It was awkward navigating the steps as a wolf the first time. Inside was one large room, a wide bed in one corner, a smaller one on the far side of the room, a stone hearth with a small fire attempting to dispel the spring chill, a table and two chairs. One chest stood against the end of the large bed. Little else adorned the space, making it a dwelling, but not much of a home.

My heart twisted up at the bleakness that greeted me, contrasting heavily in my mind to the flowers, the lace doilies, the little touches that Mrs. Hawthorne, and then Rebekkah and me, had added to our house to make it *home*.

I heard Richard shifting behind me. "I'll have a curtain drawn up so you can have your own space within the house. For now, I'll dress then turn so you can change in privacy."

I squeezed my eyes shut, still in my fur, the sounds of Richard dressing the only thing filling the emptiness.

"I'm finished. You can open your eyes," Richard said, slight amusement in his voice. I glared at him.

He nodded, left the bundle of clothes beside me, and turned away. Agonizing in its slowness and the awkwardness that came with still learning my new body, I clumsily managed to shift, clenching my teeth together as the pain of it made my muscles go rigid and left me feeling boneless afterward.

The scent of soap, forest, and hard work lingered on the well-worn material of the dress. Unlocking my joints, I stiffly dressed, shivering against the cool feel of the fabric.

"I'm dressed." I chattered the words.

Richard's gaze swept my face, sorrow and acceptance scrawling across his features as anger, despair, and helplessness burned in the back of my throat.

"Let us introduce you to your pack. Remember, you are the Alpha's woman. Your words and approval carry weight. My—our—pack has had more hardship in the past year than anyone should ever face. I know you're no stranger to hardship." He swallowed hard as guilt flashed in his eyes. "But I would ask for any measure of grace you have to be bestowed upon my people. We're your home now, too."

His words tugged at something deep inside me where the anger festered. Richard had wronged me. But his pack had not. I took a deep breath and the wolf inside me swished her tail and leaned her head comfortingly against me.

The wood creaked beneath my frozen bare feet as I gingerly came down the steps.

Three gaunt men, one waif-like child, and the woman whose cheek bones protruded from her face, stood in a line, staring at me. Bodies, broken spirits, destined for death.

Hopelessness wafted from them. How would we ever survive next winter?

Responsibility settled onto my shoulders. Springing from some baser nature, Wolf acknowledged that these people were *mine*. I would help care for them. If I didn't, we'd surely all perish.

Four days later, Richard took me to the woods to practice being in my fur. I was beginning to find the joys of being untethered to my human skin—a freedom I'd never known in the Hawthorne pack. The association did something towards lessening my anger at Richard. I hadn't forgiven him yet, but we could be civil to one another. I slept in the small bed on the far side of the room while he took the larger one. As he'd promised, he'd strung a sheet around my bed, giving me the privacy I desperately craved. He'd been attentive and kind, though I was sure some of that still came from his guilt.

We tracked along the river, sniffing new things, discovering the world through my wolf eyes, when suddenly, my ears pricked forward. Moaning carried on the wind. I yipped for Richard who also had his ears turned toward the sound.

Moving silently through the trees, we crept upon a scene that sent my gut spiraling and my head spinning. The scent of bear lingered, and Wolf's hackles rose.

A boy—not quite man but not quite child—lay moaning on the ground, his leg sliced and oozing blood onto the dirt of the track where a wagon lay overturned, the unmoving bodies of a man and woman, equally mauled and broken, smashed beneath the heavy wagon.

The boy cried out again, agonized.

Pain lanced my heart as hope kindled.

I knew how we were going to save our pack.

CHAPTER 9

Richard

I swallowed as the scene before me filled me with helpless rage. I was angry with the bear for the destruction it had caused—too near a reminder of the pack members I'd lost. I was angry with myself that I could do nothing. That boy on the ground would die. The puddle of blood beneath him was too large, his wound too grievous.

Startling slightly as Edith moved from our concealed place in the brush, I nearly barked for her to return to me, but held my tongue as she went over to the boy, nosing him gently. He whimpered in fear.

Edith turned and looked me in the eyes.

We're going to save the pack. We're going to survive.

Before I could even formulate a response to her mental declaration, she opened her mouth, fangs glistening in the weak light, and bit down hard on the boy's neck. The boy screamed and went limp.

I yelped in alarm, then watched, heart pounding as she stepped back, licking the blood from her lips. The boy twitched then was still.

Edith sat calmly on her haunches, a calculating expression on her wolf's face. Silky grey fur sprouted along the boy's arms as his leg wound began to close. I ran to Edith's side, watching in amazement as the boy painstakingly went through his first shift.

He was too young. He shouldn't shift yet, but the bite of the wolf had infected him. Saved him.

Wonder struck me. She was right. There were orphans all over these hills who needed help—needed saving. I needed them as badly as they likely needed me—my pack. Together, we could all survive. Wolf pawed inside me. I was a strong Alpha. I *would* ensure my pack's survival.

I could not lose more of them.

It would destroy me.

Edith had just shown me how I could ensure the existence of the Woods pack for generations to come. I tore my gaze from the shifting boy on the ground and took Edith in afresh. Her wolf leaned forward, eyes riveted on the boy's thrashing. Her nose twitched. A drop of blood still lingered at the corner of her lips. Respect blossomed in my chest for this woman. This woman whose future I'd destroyed and rewritten.

Just as she'd rewritten the future of a dying pack.

Perhaps I needed her and not Rebekkah after all.

Three
Autumns
Later

CHAPTER 10

Edith

We did save the pack.

We brought them back from the brink of extinction. But it left me with shame and guilt enough that even when Richard broke his silence regarding the past and offered to let me go visit Rebekkah after the birth of her child—a son, I heard—I couldn't do it. I was ashamed. I'd done the very thing I'd railed against Richard for doing to me.

We changed them.

Changed them against their wills. Took their choices from them.

Those we'd found had been dying or were left abandoned and orphaned. We gave them a home, a hope, a second chance.

That's what I told myself. That's how I justified it.

But the guilt and anguish I felt afterward let me know I was merely deluding myself. There was a reason the Hawthorne pack had a rule about not changing a person until they were sixteen. I didn't want Rebekkah to know what I'd become. It would break her heart.

The new wolves helped us survive, but they were rough, harder to control, harsher than born wolves. Richard was up to the task, but our pack was wilder than most. Even fringing on feral sometimes when the younger wolves got too antsy. All the same, they were ours. The men and boys in our pack still outnumbered the females. We needed to find mates for some of the younger men. It would help them settle.

Thinking these things as I watched through the front window as my pack went about their evening chores, I felt my face heat. Even though we were mates, after all this time, Richard had kept his word. He was no more monster than I. We still slept on opposite sides of the cabin.

But now that I'd grown, aged, lived, experienced life with our pack, I found those once-cherished girlish feelings I'd held for Richard growing again. Wolf encouraged them, too, like she felt it was time. Time to put the guilt of what I'd done behind and move forward.

With Richard.

As if my thoughts could conjure him, my mate came through the door.

"Hello, Edith. Has your day gone well?" he asked casually as he went to wash his hands in the basin.

Quickly, I closed the curtains across the window and drew him a cup of water from the bucket. I brought it to the table for him, setting it next to a bowl of steaming venison stew.

"Thank you," he said as he took a grateful drink.

I swallowed, unsure what to say.

Richard raised an eyebrow. "Edith, are you well?"

I nodded, still not trusting my voice. He held out his cup of water, concern passing over his features. I took a sip, tasting him on the rim. Wolf shivered in anticipation and nudged me.

"Richard, do...do you think you could ever fancy me?" My voice was dry and papery like an old corn husk.

"What's brought all this on?" He took the cup and set it back on the table, lightly taking my hands in his. "We're mates, Edith. I am devoted to you. Have I done something to make you question that?"

"No." I shook my head. Thoughts of the way he'd looked at Rebekkah—the way I knew he'd wanted her filled me with sharp pangs of inadequacy. I wanted to tell him my thoughts, but we never spoke of Rebekkah. It was too painful for both of us. I took a breath and forged ahead. "I know your wolf is devoted to me. But could the man ever love me?" The words ended so softly, they were barely a hush of breath.

He stepped closer, his fingers tightening slightly against my hands. "What are you saying, Edith?"

I forced myself to meet his gaze, strong and intense just like the man. "I would be your proper wife," I whispered.

Understanding dawned and his mouth opened slightly, though nothing came out. My belly dropped to my toes as Wolf whined within me—desperately wanting our mate's approval.

"I know I'm not what—" *who* "you desired," I started, tears pricking the back of my eyes.

"Edith, stop." He brought one of my hands to his lips and kissed the palm. A strangled noise sounded from the back of my throat as tingles raced through my body. "You are my mate. My wife. You are mine." He kissed my other palm. "And yes. The man could love you." His eyes twinkled as a half-smile tipped his mouth.

Joy rushed through me and made me momentarily light-headed.

"Oh," I gasped. "That's good."

Richard laughed as I felt a flush crawling up my neck. Richard met my gaze for a heated moment.

"The man does love you," he said softly before slowly tipping his head and brushing his lips against mine.

Also by AJ Skelly

For more of The Wolves of Rock Falls, check out the rest of the series. Found wherever books are sold. Each book contains a part of the continuing chronological story, but tells the tale of one couple, and can be read alone, but will be the most satisfying if read in order.

Dark Shift—Prequel
First Shift
Rogue Shift
Sworn Shift

Coming Soon:
Pack Shift
Lost Shift

Other books coming by AJ Skelly:

Of Flame and Frost coming March 2023

Read more of AJ's short stories in these anthologies:

Moonlight and Claws

What Darkness Fears

Aphotic Love

Hidden Villians

Where Giants Fall

Fool's Honor

Fantasea

About the Author

AJ Skelly is an author, reader, and lover of all things fantasy, medieval, and fairy-tale-romance. And werewolves. She has a serious soft spot for them. As an avid life-long reader and a former high school English teacher, she's always been fascinated with the written word. She lives with her husband, children, and many imaginary friends who often find their way into her stories. They all drink copious amounts of tea together and stay up reading far later than they should. To find out more about AJ Skelly, please visit www.ajskelly.com, find AJ on social media @a.j.skelly or join her FaceBook group, Readers of AJ Skelly.

The Publisher

Find other Quill & Flame titles at www.quillandflame.com
or @quill.and.flame.publishers on Instagram.